Slinky Malinki, Open the Door

Lynley Dodd

Gareth Stevens Publishing
MILWAUKEE

Slinky Malinki
and Stickybeak Syd
were a troublesome pair;
do you know what they did?
Alone in the house
one mischievous day,
they opened a door,
and they started
to play.

They shredded a shirt
and they fought with a shoe,
a long woolen scarf,
and a petticoat, too.
THEN . . .

Slinky Malinki
jumped high off the floor,
he swung on a handle
and opened
a door.

They tangled the towels
and hung on a rope,
they paddled in powder
and slid on
the soap.
THEN . . .

Slinky Malinki
jumped high off the floor,
he swung on a handle
and opened
a door.

They tipped out some pillowcases
tied up in pairs,
they rolled in a carpet
and bowled down
the stairs.
THEN . . .

Slinky Malinki
jumped high off the floor,
he swung on a handle
and opened
a door.

They tattered some letters
and battered some books,
they scattered some paperclips,
pencils,
and hooks.
THEN . . .

Slinky Malinki
jumped high off the floor,
he swung on a handle
and opened
a door.

They crept up on cushions
and vases of flowers,
they battled with curtains
for hours
and hours.
THEN . . .

Slinky Malinki
jumped high off the floor,
he swung on a handle
and opened
a door.

What a shemozzle,
the things that they did –
Slinky Malinki
and Stickybeak Syd.
They stirred up some spoons
and a bowl full of fruit
in a sea of spaghetti
and vegetable soup.

They knocked over packets,
they went for a ride;
THEN came a scratch
and a rustle
outside.
So . . .

Slinky Malinki
jumped high off the floor,
he swung on the handle
and . . .

opened the door.

For a free color catalog describing Gareth Stevens' list
of high-quality children's books, call 1-800-341-3569
(USA) or 1-800-461-9120 (Canada).

GOLD STAR FIRST READERS

HELP! by Nigel Croser
Picnic Pandemonium by M. Christine Butler

and by Lynley Dodd . . .

Hairy Maclary from Donaldson's Dairy	*Slinky Malinki*
Hairy Maclary's Bone	*The Apple Tree*
Hairy Maclary Scattercat	*The Smallest Turtle*
Hairy Maclary's Caterwaul Caper	*Wake Up, Bear*
Hairy Maclary's Rumpus at the Vet	*A Dragon in a Wagon*
Hairy Maclary's Show Business	*Find Me a Tiger*
The Minister's Cat ABC	*Slinky Malinki, Open the Door*

Library of Congress Cataloging-in-Publication Data

Dodd, Lynley.
    Slinky Malinki, open the door / by Lynley Dodd. -- North American ed.
       p. cm. -- (Gold star first readers)
    "First published in New Zealand by Mallinson Rendel Publishers
Ltd."--T.p. verso.
    Summary: Slinky Malinki, a mischievous cat, and Stickybeak Syd, a
bird, get into lots of trouble when they are left alone in the house.
    ISBN 0-8368-1074-0
    [1. Cats--Fiction. 2. Birds--Fiction. 3. Stories in rhyme.] I. Title. II. Series.
PZ8.3.D637Sn   1994
[E]--dc20   93-21180

North American edition first published in 1994 by
Gareth Stevens Publishing
1555 North RiverCenter Drive, Suite 201
Milwaukee, Wisconsin 53212, USA

Printed in MEXICO

2 3 4 5 6 7 8 9 99 98 97 96 95 94